Bears on Cha
Osos en sillas

Shirley Parenteau

illustrated by David Walker
ilustrado por

translated by Georgina Lázaro
traducido por

CANDLEWICK PRESS

Four small chairs
just right for bears.
Where is the bear
for each small chair?

Cuatro pequeñas sillas
perfectas para osos.
¿Dónde estará el oso
que va en cada silla?

Calico Bear
sits on a chair.
He likes it there
on his one chair.

Oso Calicó
se sienta en una silla.
Le gusta estar ahí
en su propia silla.

Now Fuzzy Bear
wants a chair.
She climbs up there
on the second chair.

Ahora Osa Rizada
quiere una silla.
Ella se sube ahí
a la segunda silla.

Another chair
is over there.
Yellow Bear
takes that chair.

Hay otra silla
que está por allí.
Osa Amarilla
se sienta ahí.

Here's Floppy Bear.
She takes a chair.
She's happy there
on that last chair.

Aquí está Osa Blandita
que toma una silla.
Está muy feliz
en la última silla.

Four happy bears
on four small chairs.

Cuatro osos felices
en cuatro sillitas.

Not a bear
has to share.

Ninguno de los osos
comparte su silla.

Oops!

¡Ups!

Big Brown Bear
looks for a chair.
There is none there
for that big bear.

Buscando una silla
está Oso Marrón Grande.
Ahí no hay ninguna
para ese oso tan grande.

What a stare
from Big Brown Bear.
That big bear
wants a chair!

¡Qué mirada tiene
Oso Marrón Grande!
¡Quiere una silla
ese oso grande!

Can Big Brown Bear
make a pair
with Floppy Bear
on her one chair?

¿Oso Marrón Grande
podrá hacer pareja
con Osa Blandita
en la silla de ella?

No, Floppy Bear
and that big bear
cannot share
one small chair.

No, ese oso grande
y Osa Blandita
no pueden compartir
una silla chica.

That big bear
needs one whole chair.
There's none to spare
for Big Brown Bear.

Una silla para él solo
necesita ese oso grande.
No sobra ninguna
para Oso Marrón Grande.

Look!

Calico Bear
shifts his chair
over there
near Big Brown Bear.

¡Mira!

Oso Calicó
hace algo importante.
Acerca su silla
a Oso Marrón Grande.

Big Brown Bear
helps Calico Bear
make one double chair
for three to share.

A Oso Calicó
le ayuda el oso grande
a juntar dos sillas
que los tres comparten.

Oh, no!

¡Oh, no!

Two of the bears
fall off that chair!
That double chair
can't hold three bears.

¡Dos de los osos
se caen de esa silla!
No caben tres osos
en esa doble silla.

Fuzzy Bear
looks over there.
She scoots her chair
beside the pair.

Osa Rizada
mira hacia allá.
Acerca su silla
al lado del par.

Now Yellow Bear
scoots his chair.
Will one long chair
hold all those bears?

Ahora Osa Amarilla
acerca su silla.
¿Cabrán tantos osos
en una larga silla?

First Big Brown Bear,
then Yellow Bear
climb up there
on that long chair.

Primero el oso grande,
después Osa Amarilla
se suben allá arriba
a esa larga silla.

The other bears
look over there.
Is there room to spare
for three more bears?

Y los demás osos
miran hacia allá.
¿Para otros tres osos
un espacio quedará?

Yes!

There's room up there
for all *five* bears!
Now it's fair!
The bears all share!

¡Sí!

Para los cinco osos
hay espacio ahí.
¡Qué bien! ¡Todos los osos
pueden ya compartir!

For all my granddaughters,
especially Elizabeth, who inspired this story
S. P.

For the Koobs . . . there will always be an
extra chair for you in our home.
D. W.

Text copyright © 2009 by Shirley Parenteau
Illustrations copyright © 2009 by David Walker
Translation by Georgina Lázaro, copyright © 2018 by Candlewick Press

First bilingual edition 2018

Library of Congress Cataloging-in-Publication Data is available.

Library of Congress Catalog Card Number 2008937035

ISBN 978-0-7636-3588-6 (English hardcover)
ISBN 978-0-7636-5092-6 (English board book)
ISBN 978-0-7636-9965-9 (bilingual paperback)

19 20 21 22 23 APS 10 9 8 7 6 5 4 3

Printed in Humen, Dongguan, China

This book was typeset in Journal.
The illustrations were done in acrylic.

Candlewick Press
99 Dover Street
Somerville, Massachusetts 02144

visit us at www.candlewick.com